Animal Babies

# Foals

by Meg Gaertner

FOCUS READERS

SCOUT

www.focusreaders.com



Focus Readers is distributed by North Star Editions:
sales@northstareditions.com | 888-417-0195

Produced for Focus Readers by Red Line Editorial.

Photographs ©: Byrdyak/iStockphoto, cover, 1; helovi/iStockphoto, 4; purple_queue/iStockphoto, 7, 16 (top left), 16 (bottom right); olgalT/iStockphoto, 9; Kerrick/iStockphoto, 11, 13 (bottom), 16 (bottom left); AngelaMedler/iStockphoto, 13 (top); a_Taiga/iStockphoto, 15, 16 (top right)

**Library of Congress Cataloging-in-Publication Data**
Names: Gaertner, Meg, author.
Title: Foals / by Meg Gaertner.
Description: Lake Elmo, MN : Focus Readers, [2020] | Series: Animal babies | Audience: K to Grade 3. | Includes index.
Identifiers: LCCN 2018056932 (print) | LCCN 2018058977 (ebook) | ISBN 9781641859547 (PDF) | ISBN 9781641858854 (ebook) | ISBN 9781641857475 (hardcover) | ISBN 9781641858168 (paperback)
Subjects: LCSH: Foals--Juvenile literature.
Classification: LCC SF302 (ebook) | LCC SF302 .G335 2020 (print) | DDC 636.1--dc23
LC record available at https://lccn.loc.gov/2018056932

Printed in the United States of America
Mankato, MN
May, 2019

## About the Author

Meg Gaertner is a children's book editor and author. She lives in Minneapolis, Minnesota. When not writing, she is usually dancing or spending time outside.

# Table of Contents

mother
eye

# First Days

Foals are baby horses.

A mother has one foal.

It is wet.

Its **eyes** are closed.

The foal has long legs.

The foal has **hooves**.

The foal stands up.

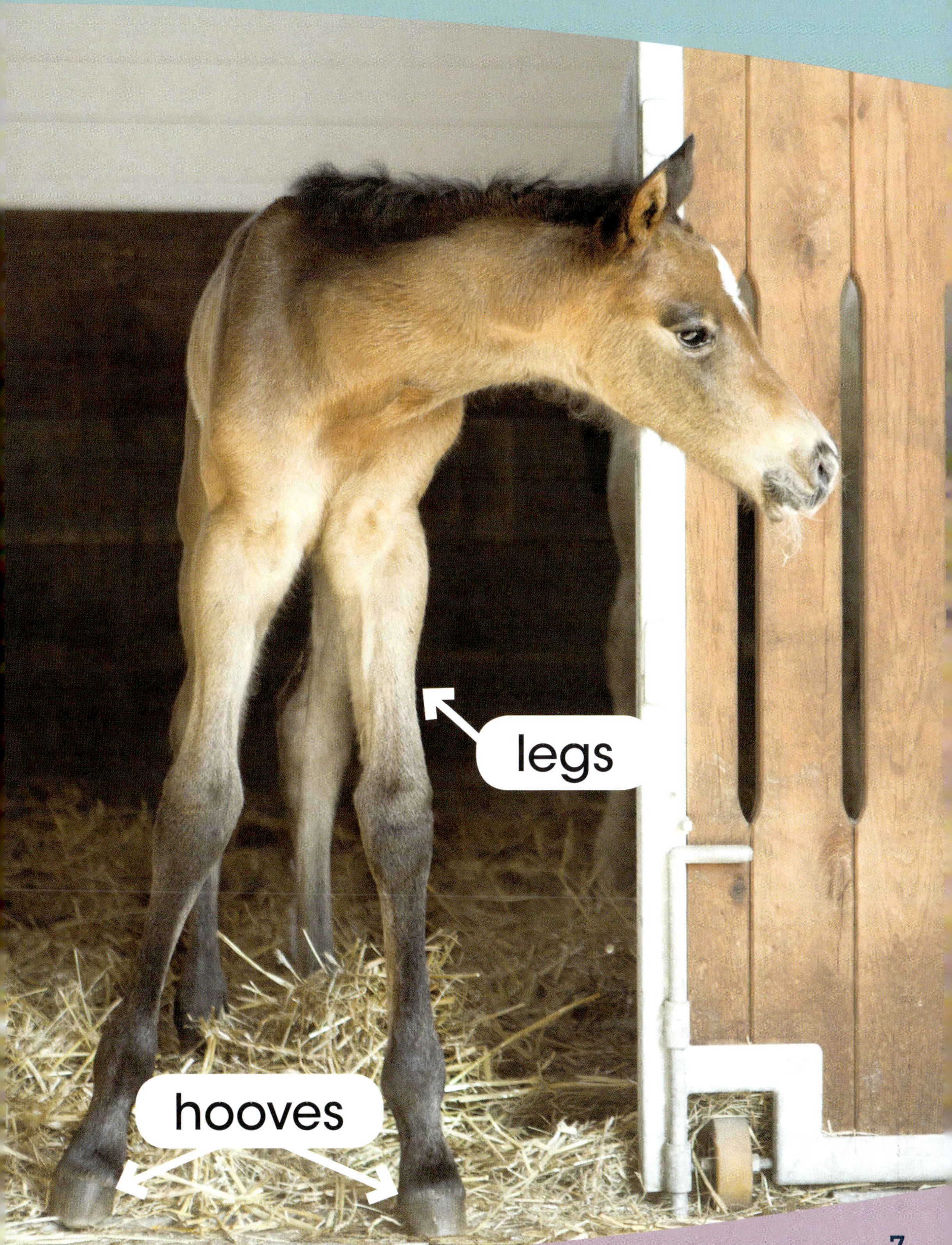
legs
hooves

The foal can walk.

It can run.

The foal stays
with its mother.
The foal drinks her milk.

mother

# Changes

The foal gets older.

It grows fast.

Its body gets bigger.

It eats **grass**.

body

grass

# Growing Up

The foal keeps growing.

It leaves its mother.

It lives in a **herd**.

herd

# Glossary

eyes

herd

grass

hooves

# Index